Kings and Queens
J. N. Eagles

Long live the queen!

- Jordan

Kings and Queens

Copyright © 2019 by J. N. Eagles

First Edition February 2020
ISBN: 9781656166654
Library of Congress Control Number: TXu 2-172-669

Cover designer: Jeanette Barroso
Illustrator: Elise Pullen

To my husband—
You are my prince charming and my knight in shining armor.

To my mother—
You are the most badass queen I've ever known.

To my life-long friends—
You are all royals.

Contents

Part I
The King

Me. A royal highness,
The finest,
First over all.
Yet, here I was at a royal ball,
Searching for the one who could maintain my rule
By winning my hand in a duel.

Marriage was a weight,
Destined to be a queen's fate.
'Twas not my decision,
Nor the kingdom I'd envisioned.
I had to marry, since I was between
Being alone and just shy of eighteen.
They kept asking me when I'd wed,
As if a king should rule my realm instead.

My future king was a charmer,
Hiding beneath his golden armor.
His heart was made of stone,
Yet he wanted to sit on my throne.
First, he had to prove his worth;
'Twas not just his right of birth.

'Twas a duel between him
And a dark armored prince.
The contest lasted nothing but an hour.
I watched from the safety of my tower
As the dark prince was defeated.
My future king, my people happily greeted.
To marry him, I was finally convicted.

I was only convinced
Because he didn't kill the prince,
But, instead, allowed him to retreat.
I admired that he wouldn't mistreat.
And that perhaps he could,
If needed, be good.

Now married,
I felt buried
Under his wing.
All my power for the king.

The king had his own crown,
Greedy as everyone bowed down.
He loved being high-handed.
I was worried about where we had landed.
While he chased his golden dreams,
I was here, stitching the kingdom's seams.

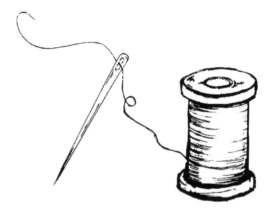

He was nothing but a clown,
Drooling at the sight of his crown.
Itching to have control,
His eyes were not set on my goal.
Instead, he wanted to conquer;
'Twas turning him into a monster.

I had to keep my back straight
Whenever the king entered the room.
No longer a monarch, he was trying to dictate.
The castle turned into my tomb
And I was a ghost, drifting through the grand hall.
No one would witness my crown fall.

I practiced dancing
In the hopes of pleasing my king.
Maybe if he saw me waltz,
He wouldn't point out my faults.
Knowing that I had worked so hard,
I wouldn't be so easy to discard.

Perhaps I could remind him of our first dance,
But I couldn't prevent his straying glance.
He'd much rather stare into his own reflection.
I couldn't take the king's mighty rejection.

I wore lovely, long, and lavish ballgowns,
Hoping the king would be flattered.
Sometimes we'd walk the castle grounds.
Yet, my dreams of his approval were shattered.
He'd bore on and on about his army's victory,
And never once mentioned the queen, I mean, me.

— to the king

Dressed in gowns, I could scarcely breathe
Let alone watch thee leave.
Thou couldn't find time to admire me,
Too busy participating in the melee
And forgetting a cardinal duty,
Which was to fall in love with my beauty.

Why couldn't the king see me as his equal?
After all, our crowns were the same.

If placed on a balance beam,
They would remain on matching levels.
And yet, he was the one I could not tame.

My role as queen
Was to be seen
Wearing jewels and skirts.
I wasn't allowed to blurt
What was on my mind.
I was confined.

— to the king

Days and days, thou would be off fighting wars.
Yet, here I was, tending the castle chores.
Thou think so little except for thy selfishness.
'Twas to thine own negligence
That our kingdom had wound up here.
Now, thy mistake we must endure.

Our kingdom had grown,
Meaning more power for the throne,
Or so the king thought.
But it also needed protection,
And not just his thick crown; he ought
To have noticed my objection.

— to the king

For, while thou were away,
A dragon came here to prey.
It roasted all our farming fields,
With naught for protection, not even shields.
It torched our homes, including our beds
And ate the animals inside our sheds.
Why did thou have to leave thy post
When the kingdom needed thee the most?

I invited those living outside our castle walls
To move and reside within our lonely halls.
At least, until 'twas safe and their homes rebuilt.
Otherwise, I would be drowning in guilt
Since 'twas the one that I had wed who caused this.
Yet, we still trembled at the flame-filled kiss.

J. N. Eagles

I wished the king would return
To force the dragon to be dismissed,
So that nothing else would burn.
Together, our kingdom could resist,
Though we had to take chances
In order to defeat the dragon's advances.

When the king arrived, he was vexed.
I didn't know how to please him next.
He ordered everyone out of the château.
He didn't want strangers roaming in our quarters,
Not all of them were our supporters.
One of them may have tried to sneak a blow.
And that, as a queen, I needed to know
Not to let everyone in and the castle overflow.
Since then, he protected the Kingdom of Benvolio.

Our relationship was now the castle drama.
It hurt my head, nothing but a trauma.
Spreading throughout the halls was gossip.
Though I tried, I couldn't stop those with a loose lip.
I couldn't even quiet my ladies in waiting.
No matter what I did, their talk was nauseating.

The rumors were more than true.
There wasn't a time we didn't argue.
For most things, the king and I
Would never see eye to eye.
He wouldn't let me be me.
I wouldn't let him rule my land and sea.

The king always left me lonely.
I wished I was his one and only,
But one of my ladies
Didn't like waiting.
Or, so I guessed.
My heart hurt within my chest.

'Twas not just the king
She stole from me.
She also tried to take
My royal ring.
It caused her misfortune.
My lady was as greedy as he.

Off with her awaiting head.
Anyone who steals from the castle should be dead.
She had committed a crime,
And lived on borrowed time.
Though she may plead, I could not turn my cheek.
Of this matter, I shan't even speak.

— to the king

She died in the courtyard,
So that everyone could see
What could happen to thee,
If thou were to take from me.

The king grew impatient
Because it took longer
For me to be ready
Since I had one less lady.

'Twas the first time he saw the flying beast,
Soaring toward the mountains, in the far east.
A blaze of fire fell from its jowl.
We feared it may try to prowl
Closer to our home, if we didn't take action.
So, the king quietened, thinking of a strong counteraction.

In part, the dragon was a blessing.
It made the king stop progressing.
He couldn't conquer everyone
While the creature's breath was like the sun.
I sighed when he called back his raid,
So that the dragon could be slayed.

The king and my knights
Studied the map all night,
Pondering how they could be victorious,
Wondering how to defeat the dragon.
I thought, for a moment, I saw a light.
I knew how we could win the fight.
However, the king said 'twas not right
For a woman to be discussing their insight.

The king commanded me
To practice my balance.
For a moment, the room was tense.
He shouldn't have commanded a queen
To do anything.
After all, 'twas I that had made him king.

I, a queen, was stunned
That I had been shunned,
Thrown out of my own throne room.
My golden seat, my power source,
He took from me. I wasn't ready for his force.
I didn't know if I alone could establish our rightful course.

I stacked books upon my head,
Pondering at what he had said.
I needed to be smarter and stronger,
So that my words would be the new order.
But, before I became a martyr,
I had to first wait for the perfect chance,
So that against the king, I could take my stance.

I didn't realize every thought
And word must be fought
In order for them to listen,
Or else 'twas naught—
Nothing, meaningless words,
And I had to barter just to be heard.

He didn't hear
Even though I sat near.
He was not the only one.
I had been shunned by many.
Although I was their queen,
They'd rather I not be seen.

No, instead I was treated as a fine jewel,
Not to be touched, not to rule.
If my destiny relied solely upon my beauty,
Then had I no purpose, had I no duty?

The king liked having power.
Yet, the control truly devoured.
With his greed growing stronger,
This kingdom wouldn't last much longer.
Because he was dangerous,
I was afraid for all of us.

The king loved his golden scepter.
He held it more than my hand.
He thought it made him a victor.
Instead, his influence thinned with more land.

Soon, the scepter would be too weak to hold his power,
If he didn't change in the coming hour.

It took a while for him to notice
That gold and land were his only focus.
That perhaps he needed to change,
In order to improve his kingly estate.
But maybe, for him, 'twas too late.

He wanted it all.
I had known since the royal ball.
But now, and with regret,
He started to realize
That the real threat
May not be in the skies.

I used to believe he could secure my rule,
But now I saw he was only cruel.
Not every royal should be king.
With or without his crown, he was nothing.

My king became weak.
More power he would seek
As if that would help us heal.
This wasn't so easy as stamping a royal seal.
He was wrong to think our crest
Could help defeat our unwanted guest.

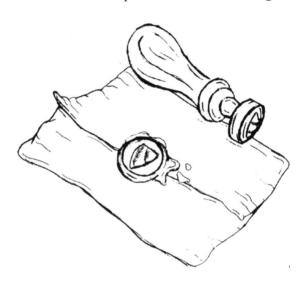

Even the king bowed down
To his own crown.
He could not be
All that we need
When upon his head
Sat the source of his greed.

'Twas his golden dreams which attracted
The mighty, soaring master
Of fire and destruction.
Though powerful, the king was distracted.
Our reign was becoming a disaster.

There was a way we could be redeemed.
To help save our rule, I plotted and schemed
To be rid of the scourge
And, for myself, more power would emerge.
We had to find someone willing to fight,
Perhaps even a loyal knight.

A mighty beast was he,
Brought us all down to our knees.
Who would dare battle the flyer?
Lest they return, scorched by fire.

None offered to track it down.
Not one wanted to sacrifice for the crown.
Once again, we were at the dragon's mercy.
I wondered if we were ever worthy.

Part II
The Dragon

'Twas the duty of the crown
To give all the people hope
That the kingdom wouldn't fall down.

However, my mind
Was on how I would cope,
If the king remained unkind.

Someday, I shan't hide.
I have lied about my power.
Within hours, his crown would mean nothing.
The king's greed may never stay at bay.

— to the king

I turned to the only one
Who was tenderhearted.
We dove into lands uncharted.
Sneaking behind thee, through the corridor,
My affection was won
By our loyal knight, thy warrior.

I used to think the crown wasn't allowed to love
That emotions and feelings the rulers were above.
The knight showed me what the king could not.
Though we were afraid to be caught,
I still smiled when the knight passed by
And ignored the king when he asked why.

I craved a new set of arms,
But I didn't want *him* to be harmed.
It could be dangerous.
The king could find it treacherous.
He could order my *knight's* end.
He could be condemned
Hanged
Beheaded
Imprisoned
But I knew this needed to happen,
In order to defeat the dragon.

I craved a new set of arms,
But *I* didn't want to be harmed.
It could be dangerous.
The king could find *me* treacherous.
He could order *my* end.
I could be the one condemned
Hanged
Beheaded
Imprisoned
But I knew this needed to happen,
In order to defeat the dragon.

The knight's attention
Was my distraction.
For although the dragon burned near,
I did not fear.
Inside the castle walls,
I couldn't hear the wayward calls.

Oh, my knight,
Standing beneath the balcony,
Whispered throughout the night,
"I live and die for thee."

He proclaimed his love to me.
Lifting a sword from his left to right shoulder,
I declared him to be my savior
From the wicked king who wanted my throne.
If he didn't return my reign,
The king I would eventually dethrone.
In the dungeon, he would be wrapped in chain.

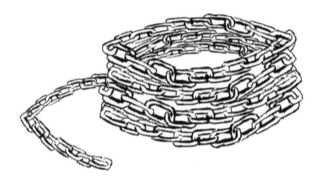

Thus, was my plan.
Though I truly loved my knight,
'Twas more important to set things right.
I couldn't allow the king to expand
And wreak havoc across my land.
We would stop him before he began.

The dragon's fire burned everything—
Fields, cottages, and parts of the château.
We didn't know what to do, not even the king.
It truly showed us that 'twas our foe.
The kingdom filled with fear.
We'd have to seek help, that much was clear.

'Twas his pride and honor that made him bitter.
The king had won the duel.
He refused to go to the now dark king, the fool.
But I am no quitter.
I sent a rider. The horse could run faster
Than any of the king's. Eventually,
I, the queen, would be the lord and master.

There was another palace, in the south.
We called it the dark kingdom.
Their rulers were full of wisdom.
I asked for help by word of mouth.
Upon my messenger's return,
I saw his face was scarred and burned.

We didn't know if the dark kingdom would aid,
But my king paced and pulled out his blade.
He put together a small soldiers' team,
Pointing with his sword, which did gleam,
The king commanded my knight to lead.
I didn't want us to part. I hoped he would succeed.

A queen could only do so much,
And I was powerless to help him.
His trial was like a death sentence
Ordered by the king's vengeance.
How could the king be so cruel,
To step on and shatter a queen's jewel?

The day dawned, and I realized
I might lose my knight to the fire-breather.
I could only keep one or have neither.

The day dawned, and I realized
'Twas fate to rule next to my king.
For my kingdom, I would do anything.

The day dawned, and I realized
A queen's heart was never free.
I must remain here and act accordingly.

I think the king was punishing me.
I went behind his back; he didn't see
That my affection had gone from him
Nor when I had asked for reinforcements.
So, he made my knight leave.
'Twas an act of enforcement.
'Twas disheartening he didn't believe
When I said he was the only one for me.
So, the king's broken heart I could finally see.

My ladies kept on speaking.
So, the king forced him to leave.
We were never good at sneaking.
Behind his back, I did grieve.
I would long for my knight.
None of us rested, day nor night.

— to the knight

If thou art my knight
Then why go off into the night?
I had vowed to answer to thee
And thou promised to answer to me.
Yet, thou are in search of the flying beast,
Which nature had maketh and released.

'Twas not the same,
To stay true to my heart
And to my subjects.
'Twas only I who was to blame,
For everything kept us apart.
I feared for what may come next.

— to the knight

I hoped the dragon would take pity on thee, my knight,
For thou couldn't see the light of our mistake.
Thou couldn't wake from this daydream.
It would all seem surreal
That thou thought we'd rule our crown city.

J. N. Eagles

the knight leaving the Kingdom of Benvolio

While looking for the flyer,
They followed the trail of fire.
It took them past many a peasant.
Their travels weren't all that pleasant
Because, no matter their retreat,
They could all still feel the creature's heat.

resting during their journey

The knight woke from a dragon's roar.
He and his men donned their armor.
They gathered, ready to defend.
Yet it flew, a battle the dragon didn't intend.
Staying to guard, so they wouldn't be seen,
The knight thought till morn about his queen.

I dreamed of an orange glow.
If I could defeat the king's fire-breathing foe,
He would finally listen and do as I say.
Or, so, that was what I hoped and prayed.

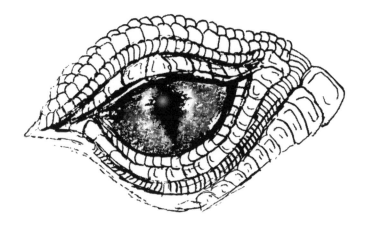

in the sky

The dragon blinked with red eyes.
It ruled the sky, higher than any reign,
Twice the castle's size.
Its royal seal was a land scorched and stained.

The knight battled bravely
For, me, his lady.
He believed I was protected.
Yet, he never suspected
That his true foe lay at home,
Sitting on the castle throne.

The king was wrong
To send his men against one so strong.
I wished he would withdraw
His military and work with me,
In order to avoid the dragon's claw.

the mountain on which the beast dwelled

The mountain trembled
Upon the dragon's landing.
Even though the men assembled,
The knight still felt stranded.
He wasn't prepared to fight,
Not against the dragon's might.

the mountain on which the beast dwelled

The beast had red scales
And sharp nails.
Its claws dug in the ground.
The knights were spellbound.
And as it crept nearby,
They shook at the dragon's cry.

J. N. Eagles

the mountain on which the beast dwelled

Trapped between the mountain rock,
The dragon blew a wall of fire to block
The soldiers from coming. It didn't want to die.
The knight ran towards the dragon
With his sword held high.
He stopped just before
And saw what the beast was hiding for.
The king and his men were more
Menacing than the dragon could handle.
But if he and his queen were to survive,
It was best to keep the dragon alive.

the mountain on which the beast dwelled

He protected and saved the dragon,
But not before another noble man
Tried to run through the flames and slay it.
The scarred remains had dark royal armor.
He recognized *this* king as someone he knew.
Though, the knight hoped 'twas not true.

In this realm,
There were two kings
And two queens
But only one dragon
To be seen.

the mountain on which the beast dwelled

He laid down his sword.
How could he kill a beast as beautiful as this?
Those who were still alive, he dismissed.
Thus, the knight became the dragon's new lord,
For saving its life from the king's men.
Mounting the beast, he flew far from the mountain.

in the sky

The dragon was not a foe.
The people realized this slow.
However, the knight befriended it,
Knowing his queen could benefit
From this scaly ally.
Pointing to the castle, it knew where to fly.

The dragon, I trusted, would soon be mine.
My king would not cross any future line.
Though 'twas not my desire
To threaten him with fire,
For now, 'twas the only thing I knew
That would force him to not stray anew.

J. N. Eagles

in the sky

The wind roared
As the knight soared.
On top of the dragon, he held.
And against the king, he rebelled.

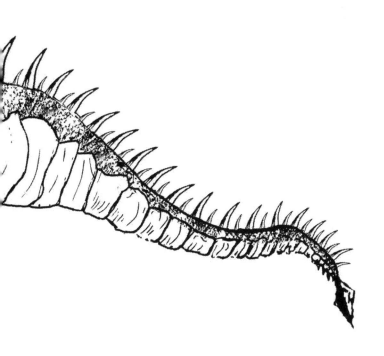

As the night turned to day,
I spotted them on their way.
Gathering a crowd into the courtyard,
We were ready to celebrate their arrival.
However, I noticed my guards looked scared.
I told them 'twas the knight's survival,
Which made the dragon not our rival.

The knight bestowed
The dragon to his queen.
To the whole kingdom, he showed
His true affection for me.

I found this gift more pleasing
Than the king's heart, which was freezing.

I was proud of my prize,
The beast with fiery eyes.
'Twas such a shame
They couldn't listen to me based on my name.
I needed a beast, stronger than anything,
For them to turn away from my king.
So, I kept the dragon around.
It worked better than my crown.

J. N. Eagles

The king's heart was filled with greed,
While my kingdom needed it to be freed.
Perhaps it could be mended. He'd change his desire,
And together we could rule our empire.

The kingdom's future depended
On how far his crown bended.

The king told everyone.
My love, my secret, out and done.
So, he ordered a rope to be hung,
Yet I couldn't imagine losing one so young.
With the dragon by my side,
The king's command was denied.
For the guards didn't listen to just a crown,
They followed the one who ruled the sky and the ground.

— to the knight

Still, the king laughed and said,
"A queen was born to marry royal."
So, my knight, we could not be together
Because, for me, thou were not bred.
And a queen, to a king, mustn't be disloyal.
Thou and I simply could not be with one another.

— to the knight

It broke my heart
That by royal law we must remain apart.
My dear knight, do not fret.
Don't allow the dragon to make thee sweat.
Everything thou had done wasn't for naught.
We'd win the war with what thee brought.

But, did it not matter?
The dragon was so large.
My throne, where I would sit,
Could be stolen or shattered.
With or without the dragon, I was unfit.
My land, I still couldn't take charge.

The flyer was my way out
Of being a docile queen.
Sometimes I had doubt.
Though it had yet to be seen,
I, the queen, would be the one to rule,
Or the king was surely a fool.

The knight warned me
Of whom the dragon had turned to ash.
Though I hoped the dark king's lover,
That I had yet to meet, wouldn't invade.
I ordered the dragon to fly for cover.

Dark thunder started to rumble.
Parts of the castle began to crumble.

I couldn't fix it alone.
When I needed him, the king shone.

He used his own hands
To save us from the ruler of foreign lands.

J. N. Eagles

By the time it took
To tame the dragon's flame,
An army had gathered at the border.
And at the dark queen's order,
She and her soldiers came.

The king told me to stay safe and sound.
I was treated as if I were uncrowned.
Only I was left in the castle when
He went to battle with all our men.
Perhaps, I should stay or flee.
But who was to guard me?

Part III
The Queen

This wasn't a fairytale, nor a fable.
Knights didn't sit at a round table.
There was no such thing as a charmer
Or a prince with shining armor.
All shields could be dented
And all shields could be rusted.
A queen mustn't let her vision be tinted
When she was the only one to be trusted.

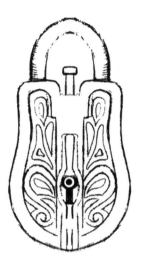

"A queen can't fight in a war."
At least, that's what the king told me.
I didn't know if he was acting as a protector
When he closed and locked my chamber door.
Watching him leave, I made my decree.

I was alone, sitting on my throne.
All the knights had disappeared.
I was on my own.
I just might keep myself in the tower,
All my power stripped from me.
I would never be free.

Late in the night,
I had a visitor come: my knight.
He came from the battlefield,
Speaking of the blood on his shield
And said that my soldiers needed me.
He gave me the key.
I didn't know how he got it,
But I couldn't just sit.
'Twas time to partake in the melee.

He slid the key beneath the door.
I held it but didn't open the latch.
Whether I go or stay,
There would surely be an uproar.
For a queen, there was no clear way.
I didn't know if I could match
The strength of my king and the dark queen.

No one would want to wear my crown.
Sometimes 'twas heavy and pulled me down.
It had my sweat and blood on it.
Perfectly, on my head did it sit.
Molded to my flaws,
'Twas chained to the king's laws.

I had carefully sewed the kingdom's seams.
Now everything fell apart, my schemes.
How could I protect my kingdom
When I couldn't even defend myself?
How could they expect me to save them
When I, their queen, ran from the war drum?

J. N. Eagles

It beat like my heart,
Hard and fast.
I wish I could change the past.
I wish I could restart,
But there was nowhere else for me to go.
I had lost the battle ages ago.

I was scared.
No royal was ever spared.
It'd be my blood
Or theirs that would flood
Every street.
I hoped to postpone the defeat.

I'd perish like my castle.
Every brick and heartbeat would clash.
It'd all burn to ash.
Although the castle would char,
I'd leave a lasting scar.
Even through the rubble,
A queen was never ruined.

So, I called the dragon,
Begging it to set fire,
So that my image would still inspire.
Though it had helped me before,
It refused my command,
And the beast guarded me instead.
To do as it wished, the dragon pled.

I wanted to be away,
Thinking the silence
Would bring guidance,
But the castle skies remained gray.
And knights kept knocking at my door.
I stared at my gown and crown, thinking
That this wasn't what I asked for.

When I looked into the mirror,
I could see clearer.
Although I couldn't breathe fire or fly,
I knew I had a dragon-like strength today
To not let my kingdom die.

I never intended to be a damsel in distress.
Yes, I was locked in my tower.
Yes, a dragon guarded me every hour.
But I had the key, and didn't ask the beast to stay here
And scare away the knights, cowering in fear.
I locked myself in the tower
To protect my power.
Sometimes a queen had to be alone
To think of what was good for her throne.

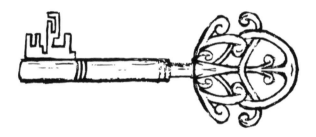

I didn't know what to do.
Perhaps 'twas best if everyone would hide,
But the king used to remind me of our royal pride.
So, I thought about the dragon and how it flew.
I could leave the king behind.
He still needed to learn to be humble and kind.

Looking out of my tower window,
I realized no queen needed a hero.
I could take care of myself, watch my own back.
'Twas time to plan a surprise attack.
Enemies wouldn't hear my battle men drumming.
They wouldn't even see *me* coming.

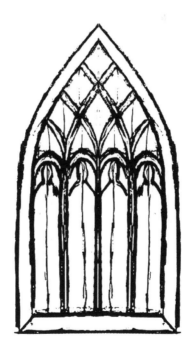

As a queen, I had a duty
To serve my subjects truly.
With the support of my crown,
My rivals would bow down.
As the power was my own
And the dragon, inside of me,
Would soon be shown.

Enough with the golden crown.
I didn't need a silk ballgown.
Give me my armor. Where's my shield?
I headed towards the battlefield.
For a queen's war, no one could fight
Neither a king, nor a single knight.

I was surrounded by soldiers
All hiding behind their shields.
My heart was weak.
Yet, I kept searching,
Looking
For a knight,
My light.
As a queen,
I must stay strong
Even when my walls crumble.

J. N. Eagles

As each guard fell,
My heart became more open.
All my walls were broken.
Without them, I was unarmed,
Afraid to be harmed.
Yet, I was forced to stay
And remain honorable
In order to finish this battle play.

I, the queen, encouraged my soldiers
To fight with the castle on their shoulders.
Through the long nights and feeble days,
The kingdom depended on this crucial phase.
Above all the hardships they were enduring,
I hoped my address was reassuring.

J. N. Eagles

— to the king

Don't fall behind
On the battlefield.
I wouldn't be able to find
Thou between all the lies
And goodbyes.
Thou hid behind thy rusted shield
As if thy precious gold could help thee heal.

My army died
At the hand
Of the queen with green eyes.
Blood soaked my land.
I couldn't let her continue to murder.
So, I stood in her way as a martyr.

I saw the dark queen for the first time.
Black armor and a sly grin,
She smelled of war and crime,
Standing on the battlefield, ready to begin.
But I couldn't strike against her
Because the dark queen looked like me.

She turned light hearts dark.
Half my army was frozen.
I couldn't reignite their spark.
I must find my knight before he was chosen.
The ground, the castle, my heart
Would crack, if she decided not to give him back.

The dark queen was stone-hearted
As if her love and happiness had departed.
I couldn't look her in the face
Because she was a ghost-trace
Of what I could have been
Had I lost either of my men.

The dark queen had green eyes.
Grown weary of all her tries,
Having lost her king's heart.

So, instead, she came to pull me apart
Because her lover, engulfed in fire, had died.
She wanted revenge and to keep the dragon's hide.

All that she did resent,
Resulted in a soul that was bent.

The dark queen had me surrounded.
A queen's resolve should remain grounded.
I had wanted to meet this rivalry,
But now that we were finally
Face to face,
I didn't think I could embrace
The monster we had both become.

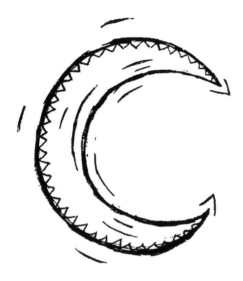

A queen could bleed,
If she didn't lead
Herself kindly.
Nobles shan't walk blindly
Through the dark night
Without a guiding light.

The dragon took to the sky.
Fire erupting from its snout,
All the dark queen's men let loose a shout.
I was grateful to have the beast as an ally.
If not for the dragon being persistent,
My life without it would be nonexistent.

Eyes lie to say the least.
The dragon wasn't a beast.
Instead, 'twas a bodyguard
Ever faithful to my regime,
Always a protector for its queen.
It flew behind the charred
Remains of every coward,
Helping the reign hold its power.

The sword was heavy in my hand.
The king asked if he should carry it,
But a queen should stand
On her own, by herself, alone
And support her throne.

I ran toward the front line
Where I found the one who was mine.
But the clouds were black
And the ground was soaked red.
My knight blinked and said,
"I love thee till I die."
I would have traded my
Own life to have him back.

The dark queen took aim
For the one who had my heart.
The strike sparked a flame
When she hit her mark.
I had to say goodbye to my knight.
Without him, there was no light
Upon this battlefield.
The old me peeled
And a new queen rose, unconcealed.

'Twas hard to believe
That I was the one to blame
For bringing the dragon's flame
And even that the dark queen came,
Marching upon my realm.
How could I possibly grieve
When I was so overwhelmed?

J. N. Eagles

The dragon saw and took me.
We twisted in the air three
Times before diving, following a trail
Of fire that burned through chainmail.
'Twas as scalding as my rage,
The dark queen trapped in a flaming cage.

Back on the ground, I battled with her.
Only one could be the finest queen.
My flaws, she thought were beastly.
So, my honor she demeaned.
I didn't want to be seen
With all these wounds she gave me.

I battled me.
Tried to be the finest queen.
I thought my flaws were beastly.
I feared my honor would be demeaned.
I didn't want to be seen
With all these wounds that made me.

I wanted her to feel my pain.
But once I saw her, already on her knee,
Proof she was more broken than me,
Her soul already slain,
I didn't want her and my knight's blood
To stain the same hand.

I stood over the dark queen.
She fueled my inner voice.
I didn't have a choice.
She must hang for her sin,
Letting the righteous queen win.

The knight, I shook.
He didn't wake.
So, the dragon took
Him back to our château
In the hopes that he wouldn't break,
Though he already suffered from the poisoned arrow.

Now that we returned to the palace
With our prisoner
(perhaps I could have forgiven her),
I didn't have a trace
Of will in my bones
To kill her.
My king thought I was a disgrace
Because I couldn't control my heart's throne.

I didn't want the dark queen to be released
Not yet, at least.
I wanted her to be punished
For starting the war
And because she tore
My heart in two.
Yet, I still didn't know
If I could follow through.

I hesitated,
All malice deflated
From my bones.
Why couldn't I kill her
For almost stealing my throne?

We had brought her to court
In order to sort
Out her crimes.
The people wanted her to hang.
But each time
I thought of her, I felt a pang.
We both did terrible things
During battle,
But she was only guilty
Of being lonely.

The dark queen was not me.
Though she might attack,
I would not follow in her track.
I was a queen that was higher.
Harder though it may be,
I'd spare her, if she agreed to a ceasefire.

I have slain my own monsters,
But only when I needed to.
Otherwise, I withdrew,
Sometimes turning my cheek.
It didn't make me weak
When I let my monsters go.

Sometimes, I still didn't trust them.
I watched them closely though.

I couldn't do that to her or me.
So, I set us both free.

The knight was gone.
I wanted a keepsake
And wished it would be eternal dawn.
I hoped it would never be dark, but forever light.
Even though my heart would ache,
Upon my breast I always wore
The key that once unlocked my door.

— to the knight

I am ever thankful for thee
And for the dragon that flew
And the king, the sword he drew.
Although there were many ups and downs,
Thou made it possible for those with crowns
(even though we may have flaws)
To stay here and make new laws.

Finally, the king let me decide
And, with him by my side,
I was allowed to rule and guide.

Although the dark queen had reconciled,
I appeased the kingdom and she was exiled.

Though I had asked the dragon to depart,
The flyer was ever-present in my heart.

I was my own ruler now.
I would not allow
Any king, dragon, nor queen
To conquer, so I would remain free.
With no darkness to be seen,
There were no enemies left to confine me.

Acknowledgments

Thank you to my family and friends. Especially, my husband, my father, Helen and Kristen for reading one of the first drafts. I wouldn't be here without your love and support.

Thank you to all my editors and beta readers. *Kings and Queens* wouldn't be where it is without your encouragement and guidance. Also, a special thank you to Jeanette and Elise for doing an amazing job on the cover and illustrations. Your artwork took this book to the next level.

Thank you, readers, for giving me the chance to entertain you with this fantasy tale. I hope you have enjoyed it as much as I have enjoyed writing it.

About the Author

Jordan currently lives in Alabama with her husband, two cats, a fish, and a hamster named Shakespeare. *Kings and Queens* is her first work of poetry to be published, though she plans to write and publish in many genres. She graduated from Athens State University with a Bachelor's in English/Language Arts and is now studying Creative Writing at the University of Northern Alabama.

Instagram: @life_onthe_shelf
Facebook: @J. N. Eagles

Made in the USA
Columbia, SC
18 January 2021